Comrade, Bliss ain't playing

Josefina Báez

Baéz, Josefina.
Comrade, Bliss ain´t playing: performance theatre text;
performance poetry; non-denominational spiritual
practice of an urban devotee; Dominican artist inner
diary.

ISBN 978-1-882161-13-3

2013

Dedicated to
My beloved Spiritual Teacher,
Swami Guru Devanand Saraswati Ji Maharaj,
My family,
Ay Ombe Theatre,
Los Constantes,
My friends
and
you.

Grammatically incorrect

Holy world   Secular prayer
Full of Clichés. Propaganda. Dancing Syntax.

Litany for my present
Soliloquy before dying
Simple. Simplistic
Journal notes

Plea   commentary   appeal
All or none of the above

Heaven   on earth   under the sky

She   it   they
        He   it   we

Politically incorrect.

Personal. Subjective. Limited.
Testimonial. Poetic dream. Fictional.
Mere propaganda.

Josefina Báez

" God, I do not know where any member of my family is. But you do. That comforts me"
Luz Maria Pérez vda. Báez
(my mother)

Comrade, Bliss ain't playing

In this precise moment, I cannot assure you

much. Dream and life, alike,

are disputing their truthfulness.

So called dream. So called life.

Dreams   I want them as dreams.

And life...   as such.

Anyway, dreams can just be dreamt.

Dreams dreaming of each other.

Before, my dreams predicted the future,

recalled the past and echoed the present.

Before, my dreams mirrored my spirit's dance.

Before, my dreams voiced all inner cleansing

and all outer protection.

Now, I either carefully create them or

let them be remembered

just on New Moon.

And in between dream and reality:

Fingerprints.

Yours

or mine.

Those recurrent, lively moments,

dreams,

day-night-mares and many others,

are sitting in the once-in-the-blue-moon

category.

Display details and desired hidden secrets.

Fulfilled or not, they disappeared.

Reality is what is constant.

Just my soul lives in reality.

And then, my all too many dreams and things in between, will know their nature. And it will not torment me when the juice is gone; while the only trace is a sweaty tiredness; while the only echo is a blurry memory; while a smile is pregnant with things that do not exist anymore.

Uncommon pregnancy, filled with not-so-fresh petals.

Let go. Let go. Let go.

Gone, gone, gone is it anyway.

What does life verify anyway?

What does the dance of life move towards anyway?

A divine choreography for the sake of the moment?

Overly redundant.

I am telling you what you are seeing.

Illustrating.

Verbatim .

Thought to word to deed.

Now that I have lived my death,

Let's get on with life.

Every single day has the entire life within.

And all that is to be lived is displayed,

in its essence amount,

in its amount of essence:

company, solitude,

fasting, eating,

public and private moments;

certainties and doubts;

laughter and tears;

thoughts and actions;

life and death,

and so on.

All in a day.

A day is all.

And a single day is so unpretentious.

It passes without fanfare.

Holiday or not.

Goes on.

It just goes on.

Melting itself in its own night.

Completing its tasks in the same silent energy

that began its life.

A night dissolved into silence.

And then,

the smallest segment of a second,

spent unconsciously,

destroyed decades of

consciously harvested tasks.

First, I told myself that oblivion apparently was

more powerful.

And my consciousness,

with nothing to prove,

said nothing to verify my obtuse, narrow

thought.

There it was:

a major teaching.

A tangible light to be guided by:

That silence said it all.

Of the many feelings

felt in this life,

identity,

and its plural, identities,

is the most complex.

So they say.

So their theories say.

So.

Imagine.

A prioritized feeling

that photographs a nation.

Flagless nation.

A nation with no flag.

A feeling that shows and tells how and why I

constantly dance

loving my black body

and my natural crown of hair.

Playing with the elements at hand.

Elements that are not my flags either.

Loving without excluding.

Saying so in my heavy accented song.

A feeling singing,

dancing, meditating,

praying.

Dressed in playful skirts and earrings.

'Cause they are playful.

Just because they are fresh and airy.

Just because they swing and shout.

Just because…

Defining itself from itself.

Not negating the other.

Me, the other of the other.

Me, feeling the feeling.

No discourse needed.

Identity.

A mere feeling.

Feelings, filling up worlds.

Worlds,

universes

as close as my neighbor.

Or, better yet, as my man in bed.

In my center,

as my belly bottom.

All possible. Quite possible.

Choices. Many choices.

All so exciting.

All not needed.

I am dying flanked by every single breath.

I am being born at every eye blink.

I have an angel.

I have an angel too. I too have an angel.

I have a colored angel.

He knows all my passwords.

My angel is blue.

My universes keep unfolding all around me.

There is one in particular where everything

is

as I desire,

as I wish.

It is not a state of condensed milk, maple syrup

and molasses over honey with brown sugar

sprinkled on top.

No.

This universe is reached while movement and

stillness are done with intention.

Total intention.

Total engagement.

Consciousness is the trigger for reaching,

with total assurance,

this splendid space.

To surrender is the verb used.

Concurrently I could land:

-in all possible disagreements

-a universe of reconcilable differences

- a live and let live

-the strongest survives or

- Kindred's souls paradise.

A twenty-four-hour period combined livable

doses of all of the above.

Even though, from time to time I might explain

or just complain.

My universes keep unfolding all around me.

Later, after life has lived,

Let's embrace death.

Until the Circle is complete.

And many, if not all games are played.

Additional taxes, fees and restrictions apply.

If you allow them to be applied...

While fishing with my tea bag,

My thoughts created my funeral.

Sadly, not a funeral with music.

Not a funeral with dance.

The seven people that I know,

the seven people that knew me,

were there.

They were not Second liners.

In general, they just had few good things to

say and many bad things to hushed-hushed

about me.

Three of them cried, cried, cried.

Fishy.

I wondered why.

Definitively not all that jazz in my funeral.

Cremation followed.

Nothing new.

A body was burning.

Like Paris.

Months passed in the next second.

And talks about intellectual property and

publication rights-talks about words and

images were tastelessly displayed.

Not jazzy.

Not Jazz.

What I call my work now,

will later be treated as some sort of a

commodity.

Commodity from the margin,

or the phrase politically correct at the time.

A product valued only after my death.

Whoever is not around now will allegedly bank

on it.

Dream. Whoever. Dream.

Scissors, matches and a clear death wish

Will is copyrighted in the worlds of truths and

lies.

Whoever, keep dreaming or let's have

the dialogue now.

Little me as well as members of the big

leagues experience this sort of things.

That's the way we develop our creative arsenal.

What?

It is unjust, nevertheless.

And my level of selfishness is massive.

Not a helpful ingredient, I know.

But, I'm still just beginning in the path.

Transformation welcomed.

In fact, forming the little self while on route.

Transformation assured.

The sons and daughters of the revolutionaries
were not present in the uprising.

The artist 's heirs are usually just passive
beneficiaries of intense processes.

This is the way we create our historic arsenal.

What?

Successors get penalized for any journey taken;
and our heroes are dehumanized by their
personal torments.

This chain of personal and collective
responsibilities needs some updating, please.

Flowers and fires are teaching me to give for

the sake of giving,

to consume while generating

this burning energy.

Posterity is a sad joke on the inert, anyhow.

A peek on the ocean marveled to evanesce.

And I am the tiniest drop.

Me as part of the mist.

Mist me.

Me mist.

Selfishness forsaken.

Of course.

That's the least.

Mist.

Just now I could exercise empathy,

empathy in the midst of personal

inconvenience.

Mist did it.

It did mist.

Did it, mist?

Once in a desert, after a Sirocco has shaken my

naturally textured hair, usual and unusual

thoughts, I read many nouns, verbs and

adjectives and just one antonym of life: Death.

Life, vitality, existence, being, living, animation,

vital, spark, vital flame, respiration, breath,

breath of life, lifeblood, life force, vital force,

vivification, revivification, resurgence

physiology, biology, embryology,

biochemistry.

Live, be alive, breathe, respire, subsist, exist,

walk the earth, see the light, be born, come

into the world, draw breath, quicken, revive,

come to, come to life,

Pro choice.

Give birth to, bring to life, put life into, vitalize,

vivify, reanimate, animate, keep alive, keep

body and soul together, keep the wolf from the

door, support your life.

Pro choice. Pro choice.

It's your life.

Living, alive, vital, existing, extant, in the flesh,

in the land of the living, breathing, quick,

animated, lively, alive and kicking, tenacious of

life.

Death comes...

And gone.

Here no more.

But there.

There!

Undoubtedly

another here.

Life and its reverse.

Another life.

Another death.

Above as below.

The proportion is always precise:

More light

Sharper shadows.

In that case we know better where the

murkiness is.

Their dance is simply our life.

What I do in the extremes,

in pain or in pleasure,

Tells you mathematically my equanimity level.

Powerful.

As when light surprises darkness.

Not even a corner is left to its dormant

possibility,

to its low versatility,

to its smashing duality game.

Bam!

Gone.

As we knew it,

here no more.

Fear is the only hindrance.

Greatness is in a constant current.

But do not call her that way.

She prefers any of her nicknames: energy,

present, alertness, honey, babe, now, that.

That.

That which tells me that I am continuously

alive!

She always sings.

But runs away when interrupted by dishonesty

or sought after by rote.

Or vote.

Runs away when the Higher Self,

the self always present,

the self that one faces in silence,

is slightly bothered.

The Self,

nor happy,

nor sad.

Life.

Death.

Just textures of the path.

"Before the real dream.

Before the predicted dream.

Before the lasting dream: the saliva drooling

man".

A title.

I have just seen you in my dreams.

And actively the night was lived.

I had you in my dreams.

What has happened now that my pillow is just

a decoration in the invitation for the night?

Where have you gone lover of mine?

Where are you making your present now?

In another dream?

In another life that quickly disappears?

In another pillow covered by prints?

Prints with too many flowers or too many lines.

From what corner of the universe are you

going to dive into a finite moment?

You see,

My heart also inquires and knows the truth.

It gallops before,

while,

and after loving.

Galloping is part of its choreography.

Its groove.

Not the only one.

Just one of many.

It helps that I erased your phone number as soon as you closed the door behind.

My heart, while loving, is still.

Still like that moment before erasing your number.

When I really knew your number.

And I allowed you to do that number on me.

Still.

Still like that moment after acknowledging that recurrent reality.

Solitude.

Still in solitude.   Dressed with reality.

Still in its rapture, I must say.

Even in silence.

Because of silence…

Loud silence.

And silence listening to itself.

You knew the alchemy of my present.

So you said.

And I thought you really did.

You said so.

Is knowledge a constant?

Wisdom is.

Does it count when you momentarily forget?

Or when priorities change?

Anyway. It was just a dream.

Neither your dreams nor your saliva

is present in my pillow.

Lesson learned.

I will never know

what the other really thinks,

knows,

or feels.

And vice-versa.

Then, to know is a futile quest

when we talk about feelings.

It is as simple as

feeling it.

Being aware of it.

Yes, aware of it.

Since it exists just when awareness touches it.

Vibrant wand,

Lasting…just the time.

That precise time when

the eyes believed themselves opened.

Glad for the textures lived.

Glad for that orgasmic, anthological moment.

It was a present as perishable as all juicy fruits,

received in all consumed seasons.

Glad for the shared sweat.

Even though I do know

that the juice happens, regardless of your

company.

Simple indeed.

Sense it. That's it.

Yes.

Sensing.

Sensing has a song within.

A song that sings

Sensing it.

In awareness.

In high alert.

Sensing Sen sing

Stillness helps. Stillness walks. Stillness talks.

Stillness sings

Sensing it. Sensing.

Stillness helps. Still.

I might also have that purple crayon,

as Harold.

Or I simply opened that door titled

potentiality.

Soon as I materialized it, I was given a second

opportunity in all decisions that I have made.

Surprisingly enough I made the same

decisions.

Now, with no doubt, I do not have an ounce of

regret.

This instance sweated out all maladies

attached to any 'could or should have been'.

A feather must feel like this.

Sweet. Sweet. Honey as aftertaste.

Sweet. Sweet.

I sing all sounds. Sounds are songs.

A tasty-singing-dancing feather must feel like

this…

Like this body without an ounce of regret.

At last, I identify the IT in all.

Then, the convent, the street, the church, the

party, the ashram and my home

are all the same.

No need to go anywhere.

Everything is everywhere.

Particularly, now that I am

my best company.

I enjoyed

and later skipped Ars Poética,

with all due respect.

And with all possible U-turns in the trapeze
granted by my old faithful alphabets and my
unending syntax games.
By the same token, after finding in many
sacred books all possible tortures, battles, wars
and human induced destructions,
I decided the way to go.

Just

one way

to go.

My way.

No U-turn this time.

No two-ways.

No way.

Just my way.

Little me
and my tiny world.

My world

and its universes.

My way.

Yes, just my way.

But I will meet other's ways.

We are all entangled, anyway.

This island do has bridges,

Shores, common and international waters

and countless other contact gadgets, cyber

talks, lines and postal festivities.

But my hyper-individualism started from my

collective living.

And so my wars

from sacred teachings.

Blasphemous? Sacrilegious?

Profane? Offensive?

You must be kidding.

My words,

unheard whispers,

do not even fan a mosquito.

They manifest just on call.

They unfold by invitation only.

Hurt is out of the question.

Not an atomic element in the intention.

Neither an option in the granted multiple

choice.

All of the above.

Below too.

And here between the two, too.

Today I see it all in its holy garb.

Not the garb used in the postcards by the

"holy" or their cronies.

But sanctified and sacred garb.

White or bright colored garb.

Holy, jolly garb.

My blue angel's dance is out of this world.

Without any doubt.

He is an angel… out of this world he is.

Indeed.

The lent space filled with my life had many

souls before and after me in every aspect

imaginable.

No comparison is just. Neither healthy.

No first

No last place

sought or gained.

Stillness sits in the heart during all encountered

rushed-hours.

I am an urban ascetic,

deciding my own temporary vows and

permanent quests.

An urban devotee initiated right here in

midtown.

I am a nun

a non-denominational nun.

A nun with benefits.

A nun married to harmony.

A nun dancing the sacred with secular riffs,

dressed in dungarees,

tightly hugged by my man.

By my monk.

By my man.

I.

If the greatest blessing is existence,

then everything under the sky is sacred.

And I do mean everything.

One thing for sure,

every routine is my ritual.

And pure potentiality… my religion.

Tite declared.

This portion of land inhabited and surrounded

by water,

this island called me,

playing duality in abundance,

knows that its water-floating existence

it's grounded,

Tied,

coupled

to the whole.

The seen peak,

this island called me,

underneath

and above

it's one.

One with the All.

So long for just surface cartography.

Tite declares.

Yes, yes like everybody else,

I am from where I was born.

I am from where I am right now.

I am from all the places that I have been.

I am from all the places that I will be.

But above all, I am that place gathering

Selected, subjective poetry

on my own trail.

I am that I am.

And here I am,

And here we are,

exercising our polarity complexes in every

single action taken.

One the reverse of the other.

Any attribute or excess within

is manifested outside recklessly,

and inside,

uttered

also frantically,

ten times over.

To surrender is my only virtue.

And to dwell in it   my lethal vice.

From here, I only see the closest.

Obvious. Physics 101.

Shortsightedness-myopia-nearsightedness.

I am just able to experience

the margin.

The periphery.

Margin,

marginal me and the marginals

within every marginality.

The only birthright inherited here is the ability

to voice your disagreement accompanied with

others living afar in another margin.

Although voicing the dispute does not mean

any step towards a decent dialogue,

let alone a solution.

But at least you cannot be taken for a ride by

other marginals or the owners of the

circumference.

You know.

And they know that you know.

I completely laid down my arms

and my heart.

And my head too.

There was nothing else.

Not even a grain of sand in my pockets.

Zero.

Minus zero, in fact.

Not even a thought.

Then,

only then,

I was fully in-charge.

Me in the midst of uncertainty.

Awesome.

Surrender does not accept partial truths,

site specific behavior nor selective mode.

All is all.

Always

for ever.

I arrived to one thought.

Induced, deduced, elucidated.

Or at the exact time when the flapping wings

of a butterfly stopped

in a far-away land.

The seed and blossom

of my own revolution.

Its strength took me from fear to fearless.

From unconscious chaos to self-control

to Divine chaos.

Back and forth.

Up and down.

And around.

Now no publicity seduces.

No promise is bought.

My rigor, discipline, thoroughness,

include heaps of

my dancing pandemonium,

my lethargic hours and

a healthy portion of self-produced disorder.

Its anarchy enjoys

the same quantity and quality for all.

Contradictions played out

not denied .

In fact all is played out.

Played.

Play.

Played.

Today's bohemian life does not only include

the usually known artist postcard.

Bohemia revisited.

Fortunately.

Now hand-made postcards are crafted quite

independently from the history of the known

waves, glitter and poses.

What am I saying? Yesterday and today

include the entire spectrum.

Every time includes all times.

Today's New moon

is blooming full

this early morning.

Today's New moon woke me up with a song.

The song was sang by many.

Many of us were healed.

Healed by a song.

A political song.

A song of a particular politics.

Artichokes. Yes, artichokes.

Beyond right, left or center.

The artichoke's politics:

Many leaves on the same stem,

Full devotion to one,

all attention to one at a time.

And always count with an exquisite heart.

Artichoke's party is my kind of party.

Antiquity as well as this moment comprises the same greed and possible kindness.

Nothing new under the sun.

Nothing new under the moon.

Human nature had it all from the beginning.

The choice is personal.

The effects are communal.

Good and evil, positive and negative, up and down, unending battle.

Eternity to play.

Eternity to balance it.

Or eternity to go above and beyond moon and sun.

My blue angel is loud. Yes, a loud angel.

He knows me so well.

He is loud just to make sure that at least I will

hear him.

He is loud while whispering.

He whispers loudly.

My act of love is

bursting out with disagreements.

And my prayer

is versed with

what you call obscene language.

God within is a poet.

Goddess within is a poet with action.

Is she a performer?

Poetic license well employed.

Life's kindergarten

amounts to more of the same.

In the self-proclaimed developed groups,

Supremacy now is dictated by a pale-color.

Other kindergartens will follow

and other colors will do the same.

Greed, ignorance to a very high degree,

will bond colors tight.

Superiority complex, masking the low selves

and their ignorance dressed by designers,

will continue to blossom.

And when their board of directors,

at that point painted with many different

colors, will keep deciding the illness-cure-

illness circle.

Still,

Love will prevail,

in the midst of more of the same.

From colors, life's kindergarten will pass on to

shapes, tastes, numbers and so on.

Halloween costumes for supremacy.

More of the same.

Love, without a nickname,

will in person, lovingly regulate.

Love will decide dialogues for the known

urgency.

Emergency rooms will flourish worldwide:

with rooms to be hugged,

rooms to listen and be listened to;

and many other goodies that will not require

money, stocks, credit cards, cellular phones or

insurance, neither certification or diplomas.

And to rest,

love will search for solitude with the same

intensity as it has danced with lovers.

At that intensity rate, love is guiding itself to be

dissolved in wisdom.

Just in my wildest dreams?

But at least in that state

Just wilderness is observed.

Another title:

"If it is the Highest of all,

it happens when All

is in its highest.

Elemental. But I will say it anyway".

My Highest lover,

like my lower ones,

wants me too when my body and my head

are at their pinnacle.

When harvest is an option.

When other options paint themselves
attractive.
But to differentiate among every option,
is the uppermost art.
At this point, a prayer is not a mendicant act.
In fact, a prayer phrased first as a ballad
and later as a rap song voiced
what I thought was my final call.
And walked me to meditation,
or another name for a daily vacation.
Act of surrender.
Gratefulness.
Charge and recharge
To lively live.
Silent prayer to articulate the vital.
The end that follows a beginning.
The beginning after the end.

That moment lived by all,

when nothing rules.

When all is at stake.

Beyond the postcard.

Beyond a flag.

Beyond any judgment.

Dogma. Country. Class. Caste.

No wonder, every time I am taken to the

doorsill of the ultimate emptiness.

Emptiness, my Highest lover's nickname.

Proven thesis : the Highest of all

happens when All

is in its highest.

My blue angel code-switches from language to

language; from dimension to dimension.

No translation. No passport.

I travel to discover more about my own self,

as any displaced –surviving,

as any traveler –surviving.

I travel to watch what I watch at home.

I take the trip.

The trip takes me.

I am tripping.

I have visited paradises on earth.

But they were really paradises on earth

because I was just visiting.

After those visits, I granted to my life its

"visiting earth" bumper sticker.

Now my studio apartment-the smallest

greatest palace is glory; my train rides, paths in

heaven; money shortage, well-thought menus

and that lover with a frantic agenda, moments

to play with hot and passing currents.

Well, my own hectic agenda was top priority in

his attraction-to-me list.

Alert,

alive,

at home,

admitting the ghost

called timed reality

and its unending schemes.

Continuing with the tourist itinerary…

if the glossy-color photo is scratched a little, it

bleeds.

Bluest sea and whitest sand beaches…but few

people could swim.

Heaven advertised for the hereafter…please

read it as purgatory lived by the majority in this

current life.

Look at the eyes of the smiley-happy party

people

full of sadness.

Anger.

Hunger.

Anguish.

Homelessness.

In few places I found amazing, unbelievable,

too good to be true order, defined social

structures, cleanness, higher taxes

and greater social returns,

nature highly respected,

impressive cultural agendas,

global warming mindful,

civic-civil citizens.

But migrants were not welcomed.

And when I say migrant, this time,

I mean working class/colored conscious

migrants.

The tour continues…

The crime suffered is the crime exercised daily.

The souvenir t-shirt bought is the t-shirt made

by the buyer's corporation.

And so is the menu and all by products.

Photos. Photo perfect. Photos.

Globalization. More photos.

Framed lore.

Tourism publicity in general could be applied

to every place on earth.

Paradise-best kept secret-culture as a way of living-amazing nature-incredible, unforgettable, hospitality plus-cuisine plus- for lovers-for kids-for all-paradise.

This publicity re-re-re-reiterates, again, again and again, the world's treasure.

Beyond borders. Catered to created market.

It's only not viable if a personal story is included; if the personal tradition is highlighted.

No cookie cutter displayed.

No cookie cutter possible.

No cookie cutter.

No.

Countries export what they need.

Saints and sages.

Teachers and doctors.

Democracy.

Artists and scientists.

Flowers and fruits.

Spirituality.

Beaches and mountains.

Silks and diamonds.

Prayers and magic.

History.

All exported goods and services are needed by the local majority where they were grown, manufactured, created.

All exports are definitively not used by the local majority.

All exports are gladly traded by self-proclaimed representatives and bought in a so–called market.

But if one person –one- in the "Made in…" or

"Product of…" country needs it,

the export is foul and unfair.

Yes.

Unmerited.

Yes.

Made in…destroyed.

Countries export what they need.

As we teach what we need to learn.

As the Miracle taught me.

As we look outside what we already have

within.

Check postcards and tourism brochures.

No locals are enjoying the offer.

If they are in the photo, the smile hides the truth or nods in disbelief at the recurrent staged performance.

Guards and guns keep the advertised paradise clean and safe for those speaking a foreign language.

Exporting souls. Exporting hearts.

Exploiting souls. Exploiting hearts.

These times…as all times…

Personal. Local.

Now magnified globally.

WWW.

For some. By some.

Just one big nation?

More photos.

New Order?

More photos. Photos. More.

I do ask, not who but what leads?

Globalization.

Homogenization.

Cards, calendars.

Photos. More photos.

Dark skin color does close doors

all over the world; including at our homes.

Hurts more at our homes.

Would that be a home?

A home where fading skin creams are more

appreciated than mother's milk.

As snails and turtles we carry our homes.

We are our home.

And vice-versa.

We are our own country.

My country is a home. I am my home.

I am my own country.

Like the turtles.

I am a turtle.

I like turtles.

I love turtles.

Like them, my steps take their sweet time.

Head out. I go.

Head in. I depart.

And continue my flight. Economy class.

At all times, putting on me the oxygen mask

first.

Seat belt at all times.

Speed. Temperature outside.

Distance to destiny. Time at origin.

Time at destiny.

Turbulences met during all rides.

The trip continues.

On the trip…

I 'm tripping

Tradition. Tradition. Tradition.

Framed custom. Framed lore.

Constant targets.

Odd tourist fallacies.

Tite has experienced.

Tite has embroidered them to fancy her day.

Like in the magazine.

Like in the documentary.

The known show take away.

A low price package with all

possible amenities

and national anthems included.

It is impossible to relax in paradise when you

are one of the supposed smiley-happy-party

people too.

But, when I hear the word tradition, sorry,

I must run to the other side, miles and miles

away.

Paradises on earth and their   traditions.

Tell me, who really decides what is the

tradition to keep if not the powerful?

Certainly not me.

Isn't tradition a live organism that includes all

times, specially the present?

Power to the people keeping the past.

Power to the people looking forward towards

the future.

Without power, I rejoice in my present.

I am my past and future, now.

I have my own tradition.

Not colorful, gold,

Picture-perfect lore.

No beautiful fabrics to die for or dances to live

by or hips swinging truths or lies.

Sending traditions include my option.

In fact my tradition of no-tradition is their

reversal.

Side A. side B. As in our LPs.

Wanted or not.

We.

The receiving and visited traditions are part of

it all too.

Wanted or not.

We live with each other.

Accounted for or not.

We Complement each other.

We want to admit it or not.

I, I, I,

I just know what I do not want in my daily

rituals, in my photos, in my craft.

I do have my own tradition.

I do.

In my tradition, breathing is the only

expression to keep alive.

And you too can testify for that.

Inclusive common sense tradition

for all and by all.

Fake it and the lungs will react automatically.

This is it.

The core.

Now playing at a theatre so near you

that you can't wait to exhale.

'Cause you will practically die.

Refinement and density are not states

sought after here. Right now.

These words dance to their own rhythm;

with their personal truth.

Erasing for good the roots of applause.

The need of approval.

This can only be a commentary.

Somehow adding elements to our unending

conversation.

Pauses and distance built-in.

Inviting the last word in.

I take the trip.

The trip takes me.

So great to love myself to the extent of worship, without hurting anybody in the exercise.

It is incredible to share this kind of love with you, in these tiny bits of moments.

With the same veneration, filled with eternity.

Love at this point is the topmost and only engine.

If I could only find another word for it;

or strip its fake peels attributed to it.

Love is love is love is love. Anyway.

Talking about self-sustained agriculture?

Love.

This is it for me.

Bountiful crops.

Effortless. Mindful.

Certification less.

Tasty.

Naturally.

All senses first.

And then beyond.

Limitless.

Yes.

More often than not.

I always wanted to write this phrase:

More often than not.

I wanted to say it: More often than not. Since I

have many often and zillion not. Not. Knots.

Nuts. Not. So many knots, that I have crafted a

macramé path.

More often than not.

Tonight I am going to read a book that does
not use even one asterisk.

"The real dream".
Another title.

Crisscrossing in life,
I too had a love once.
A dream of love.
A love dream.
The man of my dream.
It was foretold into minute details.
Past and present lives; likes and dislikes;
favorite poems; favorite food,
beginning, middle and end.
Heads, hands, hearts and hips in sync.

And you know that that's the most accurate

definition of L O V E.

The H syndrome. The H effect.

Head-hands and heart in sync.

I should start at the end.

Now that there's no nostalgia.

The farewell banquet included artichokes and

pomegranates.

Honey and almonds. Figs and dates.

He went.

Or I did?

We separated long after our time was due.

He was just one of my blessings. The ninety-nine others were pushed until his grace inhabited every one of my pores. And lover's plenitude was permanently written all over me.

Love's tattoo.

Intimate calligraphy.

Soul's way. Sustained assertiveness. Soul's way.

At the zenith of our love we separated.

The ninety-nine blessings poured in.

Thirteen years of the most complete-honest love was predicted.

Lived.

We pushed the forecast to live our seventeenth year.

We did:

Knowing the consequences, working always with poetry at hand and honesty in all actions.

Silence and words had the same weight

as hugs and kisses.

Two different people dreamt the same dream,

at the same time, in the same bed.

It happened to us.

It was the sign for the other blessings to come

in.

It was the omen sketching the goodbye.

Stillness became more powerful.

Quietness sang reasonable and predicted

songs.

Since this lover's love was rooted in details.

Our privacy was tight.

Our love was just for us.

For a limited time only.

I did get satisfaction.

Total satisfaction, as the best satisfaction this

limited body could get.

Its residues talk loud and clear.

Being well loved has giving me an ease that

I am not able to describe.

But is quite concrete. Quite real.

The astrologer who predicted his coming

wrote me a letter about his going.

Or my going?

One dishonest lover for your entire lifetime or

the most absolute wholesome honest lover for

thirteen years.

No need to wait to decide on new moon.

Right then I told you. Right now I write,

just give me thirteen years of the greatest

honest love.

The day I met him he asked me if I could marry

him that day.

I told him that I did not have time but could

squeeze him in three days later.

It's a deal.

The squeeze?

The marriage and the squeeze!

In three days we were married.

Sweetly squeezed too.

We asked then those questions that usually

take passion-engagement-marriage and

divorce.

We asked then last names and preferred side

in bed.

Artichokes and pomegranates for the marriage

banquet.

Dates syrup and rose petals created the drinks.

And tea.

Pundit John Coltrane's Ballads on repeat mode

gracing the silences.

Jasmine flowers all over us.

Jasmine flowers in our bed.

Jasmine flowers and rose petals all over.

Specially made, for us and by us,

ceremonies for toes and fingers silver rings

embellished the dusk.

A love contract was drafted:

Honesty above all

Daily physical touch

Loving more than eating

Eating more than fighting

Smiling and laughing galore

Please do not speak in your language when
I am upset 'cause I will immediately forget my
reasons with your song.

I second that emotion.

Nobody is allowed in our house-in our bed-in
our vacations-in our poetry.

My books are my books.

You can read them.

And vice-versa.

Although, his preferred subject has to many
formulas, graphs and logs.

My music is my music.

And vice-versa.

We can share it.

Versa. Vice.

My one and only love.

My dream. My love.

My dream love.

My love's dream.

My man of my dreams. The man of my dreams.

My dream of love ended, as predicted, when

the period appeared next to the r.

Good dreams wake me up with precise poems.

Pomegranate seeds

on my lover's torso.

Religion

versed naked.

When I closed my eyes, when I closed them

hard and tight. Guess whom did I see?

That dream. That reality.

That real dream truly taught me that one can' t
have all the blessings at a given time.
One of the finest options will always be to
consciously decide what one will lack.

I have lived the many ends of time.
Time limits.
The limits of time.
That second that culminated in its precise end.
And still, I could not make the connection.

In fact I thought that what lasted more
was truer.
But time cannot measure truth,
time in itself is limited.

A second letter arrived.

The arrival date was the day when the prophet of my love life died.

"If you decide, this year you will enjoy two more intimate encounters in your life; none as honest and exquisite as your one and only devotee lover.

They might even just be a waste of your energies.

They might even rob you of your present blessings.

If you decide to play, play far away from your altar.

Play without writing a poem for him.

Play without dancing for him.

Play without sharing silence with him.

Play without being in public with him.

Play without eating and repeating his name in
your private banquet of artichokes and
pomegranates, on a jasmine carpet.
The pendulum echoed your decision.
I am glad that you will not waste your energy.
Your lover's love loved your love so much
that his golden love wish has been granted.
He will come back, in another body, for
another thirteen years in your life.
This life. This year.
You will recognize him. Do not worry.
Somehow he will pronounce a verse from your
poem. Somehow he will mention his-your
favorite food.
You will completely identify his soul after the
third kiss; again not a frog, not a prince
but a man. A man of truth.

Transparency.

Joy.

A lover of love.

Your love.

He is your company for the most quotidian time.

Time before or after the celebration euphoria.

Time before or after departures and tears.

Life time.

Life.

I know that you will easily extend the loving time with your hugs, laughs, silences and poetry to at least seventeen or twenty-one years.

You have my blessings, my child".

The cherry.

The cherry on top.

The last cherry on top.

No sweat.

I already ate the cake, frosting and

the cherry included before.

I may or may not play.

But I welcome the possible he-cherry on top.

On sides. Bottom. On back too.

Yes. He-cherry on extra time. Extra innings.

He-cherry on top.

Jasmine and roses on the horizon.

A horizon delineated by dates and figs.

Pomegranate seeds to dye tongues and wake

up sublime desires.

Known but always fresh and creative menu.

An undercurrent smile now walks with me.

Imagine this ocean within.

Imagine this permanent dance.

This constant song.

A waiting that already has his presence.

A presence that met, transformed

and with whispers

faded away every bit of loneliness.

My angel.

My blue angel. Where is he now?

Have you seen my angel?

Where is my angel now?

An angel on strike, jealous or mad?

I am the chosen one.

I am the chosen, to polish a letter part of the

longest ever and ever sentence.

A humongous line with a defined period at the

end of its own beginning.

The mother of all syntaxes starts there.

There, where it really all started.

Everyone alive and living in this world holds a
letter, not the initial of their name printed and
signed in vital records.

This is The initial.

The initial cue.

The initial dance.

Life and death automatically renew the
members of the worldly line.

Life and death bestows the change letters.

Please do not imagine the Rockettes.

Please.

Far from it, the sentence 's nature lies on the
letter carrier uniqueness not choreographed
line.

Smiles, kicks and red lipsticks are not required.

They are your own call.

We are letters in the alphabets of life and death.

Death and illness lead us to another sentence.

In another realm.

In another paradigm.

But I was surprised the most when I realized that all letter holders, at the end, search in their own way for the same thing.

The sentence changes, faintly, with time.

And we see the time changing sturdily.

Its meaning oscillates from straight to obtuse to acute to right. And again, every side of the angle dancing, clock and counter-clock wise.

Each letter has many layers within.

Like an onion with endless red, white or yellow dresses.

Like the unfeasible-never-built-tallest

skyscraper that really tickles the clouds in its

route to beyond. Its elevator takes us

to the many moons and moods of our own

selves.

In heaven and hell they have the same games.

So up-down-and center, some kind of Scrabble

is encountered.

In our worlds, we always play with some kinds

of words.

Thoughts. Words, deeds.

Worlds, mirrors of each other.

I am a chosen one.

And so are you.

My life's film had been scheduled

to be seen three times.

When I was an infant,

I pretended that I was sleeping most of the

time.

But in fact, I was the sole viewer of my past and

coming possibilities.

In that first showing, intermissions

were programmed just for the usual biological

needs.

You know.

I cannot forget smiling to very unusual

expressions of love.

Few times I was caught being my true self.

"Oh what an old soul"

"She seems to understand"

"She does not like so and so"

"She was just awake.

Oh My God, she is pretending she is sleeping".

That day I decided that I would not have kids.

I was a kid myself. I knew.

Walking all these years, living, in life, alive,

I might have forgotten what my best options were.

I've forgotten pretty much that first showing.

I might have forgotten that film starring me.

But I know that my best decisions are highly influenced by that 1st viewing.

Somehow.

Recently, I have attended the 2nd viewing

Midlife.

Menopause.

Light not at the end, but while in the path in
the tunnel.

When not much is desired.

When not much is sought after.

When not much is really done.

When to tell you the truth, not much matters.

The movie has being technically updated

to a video clip format, high definition on DVD.

Divine vision delight.

DVD for me.

I realize that this is the only occasion when I will
be able to sit.

To sit where I desire,

How I desire.

This is the only occasion that I have worked to
schedule this opportunity.

That I have polished the moment with many

fasts and all possible silences;

that I have called upon this possibility as a

Divine Blessing.

Infant before,

Later a senior,

both instances with caretakers around.

Thus in this showing only, I have decided which

chair is more comfortable for me.

I am in a bus.

I am in the town where I was born.

La Romana. Dominican Republic.

My present

is that moving bus.

I am there, as I am now.

Gray haired.

White cotton-clothes.

And when I looked thru the window on the left,

I saw myself as if I had stayed there.

Eyes full of dreams.

And not one realized.

There, living the dreams that others have

decided.

And you do not even realize that they were not

yours.

Your heart is caught up.

Your mind is tangled.

And you can only voice discontent.

Jealousy.

Gossip.

If a smile is seen,

Sarcasm dances.

If a song is sang,

Truth is being covered.

Billboard ads

screamed at everybody.

Especially at me.

Specifically at me.

Telling me   telling everybody

That is not the town.

That is not me.

But me, in the town

this time and age.

Me in this body,

now present.

Now dying.

That is not the bus.

That is not me.

But me on the bus

at this time and age.

Me in this body

now present.

Now dying.

Then

No hard feelings.

Truth is unavoidable.

I closed my eyes tight.

Very tight.

The film continues…

Gladly those that I love travel with me.

They are always sitting with me

on the bus carrying my present.

Turning my head from left to right

I glanced to the front of the bus.

It was foggy.

A smiling old black woman

Dressed in white.

White cotton-clothes.

Gray haired.

Nodded her head in agreement.

It was foggy. She was myself.

I did not pay much attention to the image

I knew.

I know. I know

She is scheduling the 3rd showing.

For me to continue in the tunnel.

In the present.

In this bus.

With no beginning.

With no end.

In the light.

To the light.

Now looking to the right,

I see myself

in my many life's stops.

My many desires

Fears

Pleasures

Pains.

All the same.

Entertaining

and

delaying

the realization of wisdom.

Inevitable

Too.

Overly redundant

I have told you what you have seen.

Illustrated

Word by word.

Thought to word to deed.

Now that I have lived my death

let's continue on with

the Constant.

I entered a second and lost myself into

eternity.

I was not alone.

Suddenly, my heart decided to step out of my

chest. And He led the way into the corners of

the minutes recklessly coming and going.

Funny dude that heart of mine.

Believes He belongs to others and not to me.

Anyway, the walk stopped at the top of the

hour.

At that same precise time, I spat on clear running water; dissecting my saliva; liquefying it to light anisette syrup. Sweet. Sweet anisette.

Dropping it on my lover's left shoulder.

His tongue met me.

My sweaty torso embraced him.

Again the clock began to dance counter-clock-wise.

Wise he is.

He is wise. The clock.

Wise in bed. My lover.

Just in bed. Wisdom. His bed.

No. Bed his knowledge.

Wisdom, knows no 24/7/365 and/or leap.

Leap.

Leap out. No fear. No limits. No time.

All the time.

There is a map.

There's a map within.

A map holding the concavity of your immense

universe.

A map that forgot to put stars on cities.

No wonder the inner city does not know its

stardom. And sits down on the steps loudly

passing the fries, passing the prayers, passing

the gossip, passing the looks, heaving sighs,

passing time,

passing braids to braids

to braids by braids

behind braids

around braids.

Passing

not passive.

Weaving the map.

The fields. The present.

The history.

Braids.

And knots.

And Bantu knots.

And puffs.

More knots.

China bumps.

Knots.

¡Forget me knots!

The design is tight. Dignified.

Maps of universes

as close as my cornrows.

Tite's hairdo. Tite's x-rays. Tite's map.

I ran all the way to the end of the world.

The place where time begins-ends-begins-
ends.

And guess whom did I find?

Yes, me.

Me, me, me.

Me, at the threshold of the Event Horizon.

Where the cosmic tickle took over my
existence.

In the midst of it all,

I lost and found myself, in every possible
existence.

I cannot explain it better than versica.

I have a friend who has Rumi's complete
collection: every published, recorded,
videotaped, filmed verse.

He can even recite many of the poems in the

original and best translated languages.

Even his child's middle name is Rumi.

But he takes no notice of our own Rumi living

in the corner.

He, our Rumi,

rhapsodizes in poetry

his homelessness reality.

He swings in the subway poles.

He circles and circles around

fetching and airing his trance.

As a dervish too.

Drunk too.

In his way with and to God.

Too.

No surprise wanted.

Wanted.

Dead or alive.

Wanted.

Wanted

But still wanting.

Unending cycle. That desire cycle.

Desires and fears watering down the ultimate

possible experience.

Maybe. Maybe not.

Desire not. Fear not. Desire not. Fear not.

Desire not. Fear not.

Let desire organize the energies to continue;

and fear give you the alert bells to protect you.

This is my prayer.

I wonder what is the name for the phobia to extreme width, height and depth at the same time, experienced in no time.

It is not really a phobia.

It is the mother of all phobias.

A lengthy orgasm.

Death.

All possible butterflies coming and going and sweetly disappearing as cotton candy on a warm tongue.

All known is not contemplated anymore.

No floor. No gravity.

Sweet preludes always race up my heart.

I thought I had a phobia.

Ignorance hallucinating itself.

Climax is a possible name.

And so is self-realization.

I spat a recurrent thought.

A thought that hurt every time.

A thought full of ifs.

A thought conceived to spoil the present.

The Truth.

A Bitter aftertaste.

Anxiety prior to it.

How could it be transformed into light?

Or into a line inclusive as the horizon?

Or to transform it into a spot within that line,

grateful to be faceless and vital?

That point is a universe.

What I feel is a glimpse of consciousness,

with a universe on its own.

Fool if we think that every reckless thought,

word or action will not have all possible

consequences.

Damaging nature.

Damaging seen and unseen beings.

Animate and inanimate universes.

But nature will endure.

Just nature   will endure.

Abusive guests.

Profits over nature.

But nature will endure.

Every storm, earthquake, hurricane and all

other televised and highly profitable so-called

natural disasters began with an ill thought,

buying and selling land,

property of all.

And continued with many

lies and other pettiness.

But for sure, just nature will endure.

Circus and zoos

Zoos and circus

The United Nations headquarters should be

located in both Haiti and Bangladesh.

Just then the many councils, press

conferences, huge budgets, receptions,

immunities, codes and ethics will really mean

and do something urgently needed.

A genuine and concrete effort.

A relevant dialogue.

Can you imagine how many jobs will be

generated there?

All experts will be there.

Deforestation experts.

Human Rights, child Labor, Health, Migration.

Eco. Econo-eco, econo-health.

A humane performance for the world stage.

Diplomacy as vocation.

Inward prestige.

What do you think about that?

Look ay my angel laughing hard on the floor.

I am hardly laughing.

This is a sound suggestion.

Laugh. Laugh.

You, better than anybody else,

know their real motive, agenda as well as their

good cop-bad cop rosters, casting and

performance.

Laugh. Laugh.

Laugh about this limited reality.

Circus and zoos.

Zoos and circus.

Sundays have their own rhythm.

No matter where on earth you are.

Sundays do not have passports, visas, flags.

Nor site-specific behavior.

Sunday's language is worldwide spoken.

Understood. Even desired.

And nobody is a Sunday's expert.

I have extended Sunday's textures

to every single day in the week.

I daily dance on an extended siesta.

On Sunday' texture.

Silence comes back and forth while reminding
me somehow that it is Saturday or Monday.
Silence and its Sunday's pace.
Monday, Tuesday, Wednesday, Thursday,
Friday
Even Saturday.
Sunday has colored them all.
When I grow up,
I want to be a Sunday.

Love resides just in me.
Just in you.
The heart's mirror does some collage.
And phony needs are shaped.
Visual and sound effects included.
Valentine's-Engagement-Marriage-Divorce
days too.

Not in the least required.

For love that is…

Love resides just in me.

Tite knows.

Tite experienced it. Experiences.

Do I know you?

From where do I know you?

Your face is so familiar.

Do you know so and so?

Did you work with such and such?

Has this ever happened to you,

that while praying a fart is heard

or worst yet,

smelled?

You are in solitude.

You are dealing with your angels.

Although now their halos are stained.

Those angels are acting up.

Red colored now.

Red acting up.

Acting up red.

Nevertheless, you are truly, truly, truuuuly

calling up the best in you.

Letting your inner space invade the outer

place.

We got that right.

All eaten spices are now spelled around.

Let's admit,

the best of us sometimes includes farts.

I entered a note.

A musical note in the middle of a crowded symphony.

A shopping list note.

A note found in the messy rectangular table collecting my rounded present.

Me and my tendency to get lost in crowded places.

No matter the form.

The funny thing is that I really felt that I was by myself.

By myself while in the crowd.

Harmonious or not,

this black note is full of unchecked items.

That shopping list is outdated anyway.

On the table, next to the present note

or that note in my present,

was my passport.

Deliriously stamped by the many coming and going.

When is reincarnation an option?

I am still not fond of so and so,
for such and such...

As one can see, I have more questions than answers.
Doubting without being insecure.
Maturing with laughter.
Getting closer to my own death with open arms.
Priority is just an order, not an urgency.
The "me with me" relationship is priority.
No celebrity hints followed.

No televised fad imitated.

All other relationships are falling into place

automatically.

Interesting.

I must confess, with great pride, that the only

certificate that I have is my birth certificate.

No university but life has granted me tests and

examinations,

knowledge and purpose.

The syllabus is always in the making.

And the basic requirements are endless.

Great. Serves me well.

As the philosopher, and many repeat, I just

know that I know nothing.

My death certificate is the only diploma

pending.

And I will not be present for the

commencement.

Great. Well served.

Lately, I have been erasing the hollow paths

leading to the past.

Leading to the future.

Hope was in line.

Hope was ego-grown. False promise.

Known surprise.

Hope brought more stress than the BQE

during rush hour.

A more laughable security than a policeman

anywhere in the world.

Shaky grounds.

Uncalled extended thoughts.

Unending.

Hope circles.

Like that, unending, hope is an excuse.

Hoping. Hopping. Hoping.

Will a 5th hoping close the circle?

Hoping.

Deleted. Gone.

Gone is my hope.

No hope for me.

Why hope?

Why not?

If hope is balanced…

If hope is part of the path…

I hope. And hop to continue.

As an unending excuse…

Hope is not even close to assurance

but to a partial belief.

Believing in a hope.

Living by hope.

Not at all secured.

You will not hope for death.

Death is an assurance.

No doubt.

For sure.

Uncertainty is not even a possibility.

Death for sure is coming.

You hope me   you hope me not

All.

Nothing.

Now. All now.

Hope anyone?

Everyone hopes. Any one hopes.

Go figure.

Fool if we think that every thought, word or

deed will not touch every aspect of our

different bodies.

Every absence of ease starts there.

Every disease stars there.

But illness would not touch our souls.

Illness would not either cause death.

Death is a whole different subtle song.

Even with diseases very close by,

the soul will prevail.

Abusive hosts.

Fantasy over reality.

But our soul will endure.

Just our soul will endure.

What can happen if harmony gets upset?

I just realized another evident premise.

Not all questions have answers.

Not for lacking information.

Not for lacking the exquisite unending

word play.

Dance of the thoughts,

perspective perspicacity.

You know what I am saying.

In fact, their nature is just to question.

Like me, years before,

heavily infused by age, written words

and all too many disqualifying statements.

The question that I do not want an answer to,

I ask it in silence.

Dances that I do not want others to dance, I
dance them in solitude.

I have been migrating since birth.
In fact, migration first comes visible exactly
at birth.
As a matter of fact, nine months
before my happy birthday to me,

to her, to him, to them,

to here, to there,

I was migrating too.

Migrating from a place with no time

and colorless passport,

to a place with no time and colorless

passport.

For nine months and some days, I was seeing
multiplying cells in my mothers' IMAX womb.

Birth day they call it.

Day of birth.

That's a fact.

Optimum migrare. Sounds latin. Ah!

Migrant. Migrate.

Migrant migraine.

Migrant. Migrate. Migraine.

Migraine, my grains.

My grains in greener pastures.

Sounds familiar ah!

Migration rapidly wrapped all my existence.

I move from second to minutes to hours to
days to weeks to months to years and years
and years. Migrating every day.

Day to night.

Night to day.

To too many places I have arrived.

From many places I have left.

Heaven, purgatory or earth.

All ask the same questions:

Where are you from?

When are you leaving?

Where are you going?

Like if a "place" would be the thing.

What about if I tell you that

I am that place –

where I am,

come from ,

and will definitively leave.

I really can't tell you

anything out of this world.

Indeed, I keep saying, consciously,

simplistic,

simple,

repetitive words,

all from this world.

Here, now, today.

Again and again.

Plain as quotidian richness.

Dazzling.

My world is ...

Is the world of my Father.

Is the world of my Mother.

My world is this world.

My world has all galaxies.

The Milky Way.

Chocolate-covered- Way.

Creating.

Preserving

And ending

Powered by my powerful remote control:

My thoughts.

My heavenly family has been cloned and

descended.

They are here.

You are here.

My world, this world,

Is my heaven.

Is my hell.

Plentiful. Nothingness.

Divinely different.

Differently Divine.

Complete with all its omitted options.

The path between those extremes is real life.

This is the most cherished instance; less

photographed

too.

While I perform my daily duties;

When recompense is intangible.

Pavlov's dog not for hired.

My world is this world.

And I am so glad.

I have wasted my energy in chronometry,

horometry, chronology, horology; counting

dates and passing eras. Finally I have arrived at

the beginning. ¡¡Eureka¡¡

The gift.

The present.

Full of past and future.

Bringing it all to now.

It is just a wise delight.

It is tasty. A juicy tasty moment.

If I should tell you one truth.

At least one.

Count on my contradictions.

Before my thoughts, I was God. Yes, I was a
very funny Goddess wrapped around in my
own energy.
Not presumptuous. And not even with an
ounce of attitude.
At that point that is.
A speck. I was a speck. A dot. A point. *Tochka*.
A mere point with the entire universe within.
All alive. All alert.

All was the void.

All was nothing.

Empty. Emptiness.

And that is all.

All.

All is where Bliss resides.

With no zip codes or sidewalks.

Bliss' permanent address has no floor.

And for Bliss, permanence means continuing-

perennial-forever and ever eternal, everlasting,

ever-living, ever-flowing, continual,

sempeternal, endless, without beginning,

unending, never-ending, ceaseless, incessant,

uninterrupted,

deathless,

birth less,

no happy birthday to me, to you, to her, to

them.

Birthless.

Immortal, interminable,

having no end, unfading, evergreen, ever-

rainbow, immortal, imperishable.

I meant to tell you that Bliss ain't playing.

Bliss creates all the playing.

Bliss is the play.

Wishing you a very blissful day!

This is a recording.

I lost my angel.

I am blue.

If I were an angel…

If I were an angel,

right now I will be a blue angel.

And blue angel case solved!

But…

I have talked more than what I have done.

If I have done at least half of what I have

talked…

Talk and deed must be together.

Deed first.

And talk would be happy as a thought.

In the best of times, thought will await its

quality to be defined first.

Fewer and better thoughts indeed.

Optimum deeds.

Sharp and precise.

What is really needed?

Vital?

What fills the void?

The void.

The void itself.

The void knows

She is all.

I perceived

this and that

with sense,

just because I thought and later said so.

And I said so,

painted with a personal history.

Before, I was guided by unknown characters,

owners of sins and pardons.

Importance has been as subjective as my good

name.

Scientific evidence suggests,

but has never been able to prove anything.

101.

One or one.

One or the other.

Science has yet to be neutral and color blind.

I assure you.

Closed to my heart, cysts-tumors-cysts

encapsulated all past grieve.

A distinctive light grew all around it.

Little by little.

I got out of my lassitude.

Little by little too.

Not a miracle. But everyday wonder.

Mammography has been one of the main

offenders.

No. I am not in a tangent this time.

It is just how I feel.

Flat-ironed tumors break open.

And of course the malignancy spreads.

Benignity under that kind of aggression will

turn sour, if not in your breast in your head or

heart.

For real, mammography is the greatest failure

and profit making of conventional medicine for

or against women.

No. I have no scientific proof. No.

I do not need them.

The pain testifies every time.

And it lingers for years.

I say it again: Science has not been neutral nor

colorblind.

Hurt could not cure.

At least no me.

My heart firmly told my body to stop the

nonsense.

No diseases are allowed now.

Die if you need to.

But illness drama is not needed.

Healing happened first on my wounded heart.

The essence of flowers adorned and paved

emotions as smooth as they could get.

Then my body raised itself up to dance cheek

to cheek with flower essence.

Dressed up and all.

That's a very poetic cure.

That's a very romantic ballad.

In alertness.

With sharp wittiness.

With really gentle tender loving care.

Life now plays with light.

Life dances with differences and agreements in the land of the possible.

Somehow or the other the entire existence is getting its way inside me.

Or I just realize the possible astonishing tenant?

There will be a moment when there is no more excuse to look out. No one named creator, guilty, precious more than my own guts.

Light. Light. Light.

More light is called.

More light comes.

More light is given.

More light is received.

Still, too much talk from this end...

At last, there are physicists poets.

Poets in physics.

Poets of physics.

They call their poetry Quantum energy.

Letters   electrons or neutrons.

waves or particles.

They too play with all possible times

and spaces.

Only just with these poets, my Grandmothers'

God feels at home as an equation,

As an experiment,

As an experience.

As the void.

Yes, they call Quantum energy

To whom my grandmothers adored as All

Mighty God.

Me?　　I call it Supreme.

And my Spiritual Teacher knows it as

Supreme Consciousness.

But his experience is not mere knowledge.

His

is Wisdom.

Wisdom acquired by experience.

The experience of Quantum,

Leaping entangled,

in all possible places,

at all times,

all the time.

Realization with capital R.

Recognizing that immense little light inside

and....

Knowing that is yours.

Knowing that it is shining.

Letting it shine,

Let it shine, let it shine.

All the time.

Every time.

Here he is!

My hide-and-seek playing angel.

My blue angel.

All partitions proved themselves limited.

East and West,

With their violent blessing

and decadent wealth.

North and South,

king and servant.

So called first, Second

or Third World,

rightly intoxicated with missing links and stolen

rights.

And the overdose of use-reuse-recycle abuse

anguish.

And in the center

Me.

You.

Gladly.

Naked of traditions or flags.

Our divine right

is urgently translated in this latitude as

humane.

Detached from all past, present and possible

isms.

Basic rights are basic prayers.

Shelter, food, health, education, self-culture.

Active prayers. Honest prayers.

Prayers not yet written neither property

of any religion.

Collectively we are praying

not even at a remedial level.

Nobody to go to.

Nobody to look up.

Nobody to pray to.

Again.

It is just me.

Not bad.

I really enjoy my company.

I certainly can live with myself.

At this point, this is well-proven-demonstrated-verified. With no doubt.

But before silence sat in,

a monosyllabic sound was mumbled.

You were already in silence.

I was drowning still in words.

I could not help but smile at myself.

Laugh with myself.

And cry for myself.

I remember the silence out of fear.

Silence of ignorance.

Silence by omission.

Silence by violence.

Silence by anger.

Silence when the memory denied access.

Silence when a mere cold wrapped my chords around.

Silence selected as my own choice.

Silence.

Silence my power.

Silence.

Many silences.

Complicity.

Not compromised.

Untouched.

Detached.

All had silences.

And I had all of those silences.

And you came with words that I did not hear.

That you did not pronounce.

You came to

induce me to silence.

Granting silence.

Bestowing solitude.

My own.

You came to persuade me to silence.

My own.

Silence of the highest caliber.

Silence that does not hurt.

Silence in the midst of all noise.

Powerful silence.

My own.

You came

to invite me to silence

or the beginning of sound.

You   silenced yourself

You   silenced   itself.

I could not help but love you.

Adore you. Silence.

I adore you all right.

All left. All center.

I adore you.

Or learn your way of loving.

Real loving.

Constant loving.

In silence.

In silence we are one. In silence we are one.

One is in silence oneness.

One is.

Is in

In silence.

Silence Oneness.

One is

Is one

One is

Is in

In is

In silence

Silence in

Silence oneness

Oneness silence

Silence oneness

One is in silence oneness.

It is so true,

In the precise moment of love there is silence.

And in silence we are alone.

Alone together too.

We   is just you.

We   is just me.

In fact, solitude dresses silence up.

And vice-versa.

Up silence dresses solitude, fact in.

Versa-vice.

With no virtue. With no vice.

Vice-versa

Always vice-versa.

And if words are said,

They are not heard.

They too are said out of ignorance.

I never wanted to lose my silence.

Silence is my most powerful weapon.

My powerful sound.

It is the beginning and end of my voice.

I never want to lose my silence.

Non-negotiable. Silence.

Is silence a path or its texture?

Now I am eternally married to you,

Silence.

In life and death.

Silence.

Life silence. Dead silent.

What really happens to time and space in

silence?

Words do get in the way.

Specially when talking about silence.

Obviously.

So many times I have said that it was my

conscience that talked; that my conscience led

me to decide this or that.

But my conscience reacts with silence and

stillness

to all.

To all

she reacts with silence.

Pristine silence.

Crafted silence filled with all sounds.

And to all she reacts with Stillness.

Stillness containing all movements.

Was I hearing voices then?

I did.

I heard voices before I met Silence.

And from Silence I go to…

My voice

My voice is full of silences.

In silence I exercise all my power.

Walking hand in hand with you,

Silence.

In your greatness, the ordinary eye does not

even notice you, Silence.

That's the only reason why they call me the

widow

in

silence.

Silence 's widow.

And the souls of all widows dance

the epitomy of silence.

Souls in a sole dialogue.

From silence to silence.

A ping-pong ball covered by purple clouds.

Volleying just a gesture from side to side.

From here to eternity.

From here to beyond.

From up-there to right here.

Pauses in between.

Pauses within silence.

It does have a rhythm that extends all grace

notes.

Pacing the song of silence.

In silence I found…

more silence.

Silence…

I cannot describe our bond,

Bliss is the closest.

My rapture   my surrender

Give hints of the affair.

My constant walks with you ground us.

Grounds me.

You,

Silence,

my constant companion.

And that precise moment

when there's not a thought.

When there is nothing.

Plentiful nothingness.

And I have it all

Silence is the highest art.

The heart of my craft.

The craft of the heart.

Now I know that the journey

Is The Constant.

The truth of it all

is that

I am silence.

I am silence

while aware of the Highest.

Thus I adored, married and widowed

my own self.

The highest of me,

that is.

That part of me

that is Supreme.

Thanks God!

Thanks Goddess¡

Thanks. Thanks.

My words have become wiser than my deeds.

The only way to balance this sad affair,

Yes I hear you.

Silence.

Josefina Báez (La Romana, Dominican Republic/New York) writer, actress, director, devotee. Directs Ay Ombe Theatre (since April 1986). Alchemist of Performance Autology (creative process devoted to the physical and mental health of the doer). Other books by Josefina includes Dominicanish, Como la Una, Levente no. Yolayorkdominicanyork, A dominicanyork in Andhara, Why is my name Marysol?